# BUBBLE GUM Brain™

**Ready, Get Mindset...** **GROW!**

# Activity & Idea Book

the Power of YET

published by

★ NATIONAL CENTER for
YOUTH ISSUES

# Introduction

According to Carol Dweck (*Mindset*, 2006) a growth mindset is the understanding that we can develop our intelligence and abilities. Research has shown that to develop a growth mindset, one must work hard, set high expectations, develop resiliency, become more open-minded, and learn to persevere in the face of struggle. Having a growth mindset is beneficial to all people in contexts from education to the workplace, to developing interpersonal relationships, to how our children will one day raise their own children.

These activities are designed to help teachers, school counselors, and parents cultivate and expand the bubble gum brain that exists in all of us. We hope you enjoy doing the activities as much as we have enjoyed creating them!

BEST,
Julia Cook and Laurel Klaassen

> *You cannot teach a child to peel off their bubble wrapper if yours is still intact! 1...2...3...get ready to peel!*
>
> – Julia Cook

**Summary:** A supplementary teacher's guide for *Bubble Gum Brain*.
Full of discussion questions and exercises to share with students.

Written by: Julia Cook • Contributing Editor: Laurel Klaassen • Illustrations by: Allison Valentine
Published by National Center for Youth Issues
Printed in the U.S.A. • February 2024

NATIONAL CENTER for YOUTH ISSUES

P.O. Box 22185 • Chattanooga, TN 37422-2185
423.899.5714 • 866.318.6294 • fax: 423.899.4547 • www.ncyi.org
ISBN: 9781937870454
© 2017 National Center for Youth Issues, Chattanooga, TN • All rights reserved.

# Bubble Gum Brain Oath

*I want to have a bubble gum brain! I am peeling off my wrapper so my brain can grow. I am making a choice to develop my intelligence and abilities by stretching my brain each day.*

**I WILL:**

- ***Expect the best*** *of myself*

- ***Work hard*** *and try new things*

- ***Become more resilient*** *by sticking with it, even when I want to give up*

- ***Be open-minded*** *and look at new learning as an adventure*

- ***Be GRITTY***

# Grow Your Brain

## OBJECTIVE

Students will recognize that in order to develop a growth mindset, you must expect the best from yourself, work hard, become more resilient, be open-minded and have grit (never give up!).

### MATERIALS NEEDED
- Soil
- Styrofoam cups
- Radish or other small vegetable seeds
- Water
- Soil fertilizer properly mixed with water (i.e., Miracle Grow)
- Eye dropper
- Access to sunlight
- Cardstock to set plants on

## DIRECTIONS

1. Discuss as a class the importance of having a growth mindset and how having a growth mindset requires certain ingredients. Explain how growing your mind compares to growing a seed. To get the most growth you must have all of the ingredients.

2. Pair the following up (write on the board):
   **Seed =** your brain
   **Styrofoam Cup =** expecting the best from yourself
   **Water =** working hard
   **Soil =** GRIT (never giving up)
   **Sunshine =** becoming more resilient
   **Soil Fertilizer =** being open-minded

3. Pass out all materials to each student. Choose 10 students at random, and take back one of their five ingredients (cup, water, soil, sunshine, or fertilizer). If a student is short one ingredient, have them write what is missing on their cardstock (i.e. "Missing fertilizer (open-mindedness)").

4. Have students fill each cup ¾ full of soil (can mound the soil on cardstock if not using cups).

5. Make a 1 1/2" hole in the middle of the cup.

6. Place one seed into the hole, then add two drops of fertilizer and cover with soil.

7. Sprinkle with water so that soil is moist but not too wet.

8. Place in a sunlit area (window sill or outside).

9. Water as needed and monitor growth for one week.

## CONCLUSION

Compare the growth of the plants that had all five elements to those that were planted without one of the five elements. Explain to students that to really grow your brain and develop a growth mindset, you need to have all of the ingredients (working hard, expecting the best from yourself, being open-minded, becoming more resilient, and having grit.) Leaving out just one ingredient can make a huge difference!

# Write Myself A Letter!

## OBJECTIVE

Students will identify times in their past when they had a fixed mindset and how that situation could have played out differently if they had practiced growth mindset thinking.

## MATERIALS NEEDED

- Chalkboard or white board
- Copy of *Write Myself a Letter* or blank notebook paper for each student

## DIRECTIONS

1. As a class, brainstorm situations that demonstrate using a fixed mindset and write them down on the board. Keep in mind these situations can be both experienced and/or observed. Ideas might include:
   - Learning something new (a sport, a new math concept, riding a bike, etc.).
   - Completing a project but not doing very well on it.
   - Experiencing a change (new school, new friends, etc.).

2. Have students think about a time in their past when they demonstrated a fixed mindset (hopefully the generated list on the board will inspire a memory).

3. Have students share their experiences with a partner or in a small group.

4. Brainstorm with their partner(s) what they could have done differently if they had practiced growth mindset thinking.

Using the information above, have students write a letter to their younger selves. The letter should be written as if the student has not yet experienced the event. Have the students explain in the letter what they can do to avoid a fixed mindset outcome.

## EXTENSION

Have students write a letter from their older selves explaining ways they will need to practice growth mindset thinking during the school year or when learning new skills.

# Fill the Bubble Gum Machine

## OBJECTIVE

Students will identify times when they see others in the class practicing growth mindset.

## DIRECTIONS

**MATERIALS NEEDED**

- Gumball machine or clear jar
- Jar of gumballs

1. Be sure students understand the difference between a fixed mindset and a growth mindset.

2. List examples of growth and fixed mindset on the board.

3. Explain to students that they are all going to be on Mindset Patrol. To do this they will help each other practice a growth mindset approach in the classroom. When students see or hear someone exhibiting growth mindset, they can let the teacher know and a gumball is added to the jar. If a student sees someone exhibiting a fixed mindset, they can "call them on it" and encourage them to change their thinking! If their mindset changes, a gumball can be added to the jar.

   NOTE: Gumballs are never extracted from the jar.

4. When the jar is full, have students brainstorm, select, and vote on a class reward. Rewards may include: extra recess time, free choice time, eating lunch in the classroom, chewing the gum and spitting it out before end of class (if school allows gum), playing board games, lunch outside, a popcorn party, healthy snack pot luck, etc.

# Measuring My Success!

## OBJECTIVE

Students will set a S.M.A.R.T. goal and work to achieve it.

## DIRECTIONS

1. Have students identify a S.M.A.R.T. GOAL they would like to achieve.

2. Set aside a time daily (2-4 min.) for students to record information on the S.M.A.R.T. GOAL SHEET and continue this for 5-6 weeks.

3. Once a week, allow students to pair/share how they are doing with their goal. Partners should work together to encourage one another to keep working toward meeting the goal. They should also problem solve what can be done differently if they aren't seeing success.

4. Remind students weekly about the need to maintain a growth mindset, even when they see setbacks or no progress. How can they tackle the problem differently? Are there other people who might be strategic partners in accomplishing the task? Encourage resilience. Though they might not see success at first, by adapting and staying consistent, they can achieve the goal.

4. Mark progress on a progress chart that is located in a highly visible area of your classroom.

**Optional:**

At the end of the project, have a party to celebrate the students' accomplishments. If fitting, invite parents and have several students present their goal and what they accomplished over the timeframe.

## MATERIALS NEEDED

- S.M.A.RT. Goal Sheet for each student (see next page)
- Classroom progress chart that shows starting point and ending point

# S.M.A.R.T. GOAL

## SPECIFIC : MEASURABLE : AGREED UPON : REALISTIC : TIME BASED

MY S.M.A.R.T. GOAL IS: _____

NAME: _____

| SMART GOAL | DESCRIPTION OF EACH PART OF MY S.M.A.R.T. GOAL |
|---|---|
| SPECIFIC | |
| MEASURABLE | |
| AGREED UPON | |
| REALISTIC | |
| TIME BASED | |

- - - - - - - - - - - - - - - - - - - - - - - - - - - - - - - - - - - - - - - - - - - - - - - - - - - - - - - - - - - - - - - -

## How I measure my S.M.A.R.T. GOAL:  (EXAMPLE)

**GOAL:**  *I want to improve my archery score.*

| DAY/DATE | TIME PRACTICED | ACTION TAKEN (drills, etc) | LEARNING FROM OTHERS | SCORE |
|---|---|---|---|---|
| **MON.** | 60 min. | 60 | Tips from Coach on stance | 138 |
| **TUES.** | 30 min. | 30 | Practiced hitting line | -- |
| **WED.** | 60 min | 60 | | 145 |
| **THURS.** | 30 | 0 | Watched tutorial video | -- |
| **FRI.** | 60 | 60 | Tips on site | 148 |

**Other ways to show progress:**
Create a graph or video yourself to show before and after outcome or product (cooking, art, playing a song on an instrument, scores or grades in school, etc.).

# My Bubble Gum Brain Bag

## OBJECTIVE
Students will use objects to recognize and explain times when they have used a growth mindset.

## DIRECTIONS
1. Pass out a bag to each student.

2. Using markers and/or crayons, have students label and decorate their bags creatively with their names and the words "My Bubble Gum Brain Bag".

3. Have students take their bags home and fill them with five items that represent how they have used their bubble gum brains ( i.e., a paper with a good grade on it, a video game they have mastered, a picture of a puzzle they completed, music they have learned to play, etc.) and bring back to school the next day.

4. Gather students in a circle on the floor, and have them take turns taking one item out of their bags and telling why/how it represents using their bubble gum brain.

5. After all items are out of the bags allow students to comment/discuss the items that have been shared.

6. Talk with students about how memories of achievements can motivate us when we go through hard things. The items in their bags represent moments in their lives when they used a growth mindset and the "Power of Yet" to overcome a challenge.

# Great People Make Great Mistakes!

## OBJECTIVE

Students will understand that making mistakes leads to learning opportunities.

**MATERIALS NEEDED**

- Interview sheets (four worksheets per student)
- Pens or pencils
- Poster paper
- Markers

## DIRECTIONS

1. Have students pair up with a classmate and interview each other using the interview sheet.

2. Ask students to think of three people they know well personally who are successful in what they do and interview them using the interview worksheet (this can happen over a weekend or matter of days).

3. Have students review all four interviews and write responses on the poster paper and look for similarities. Discuss any common trends: what do successful people understand about failure? How did a growth mindset help them achieve their goals? Were there examples of times when a fixed mindset caused them setbacks?

4. Allow students to share their findings with the class.

5. On the other side of the poster board, have each student summarize their experience of this activity with a picture or a quote.

# Making Great Mistakes Interview Sheet

INTERVIEWER NAME:_____

INTERVIEWEE NAME:_____

1. **In your opinion, what are some of your talents?**

   _____

   _____

   _____

2. **From the list above, what do you consider to be your greatest talent?**

   _____

   _____

3. **While developing this talent, what are memorable mistakes you made along the way?**

   _____

   _____

4. **Did making these mistakes help you grow? If so, how?**

   _____

   _____

5. **Have you ever felt like quitting?  Why?**

   _____

   _____

6. **What encourages you to keep going when you get discouraged?**

   _____

   _____

7. **Who in your life has taught you the most and why?**

   _____

   _____

8. **Why do you think making mistakes is important?**

   _____

   _____

# The Bubble Gum and the Spoon!

## OBJECTIVE

Students will experience the benefits of practice and repetition.

## DIRECTIONS

1. Divide class up in teams of four.

2. Pass one spoon out to each student and have them write their name on the handle with marker.

3. Set up an obstacle course that involves passing the gum from one spoon to the other with spoon handles in the kid's mouths.

4. Time the first run of the obstacle course. For each instance the gum is dropped, add five seconds to the time for that team.

5. Have students discuss as a team and class the challenges that were confronted in the first run. What mistakes were made? What did you learn from these mistakes? What ideas can you come up with to help your team make less mistakes? Write down responses for future reference.

6. During the next week, schedule 10 organized practice sessions with the spoons and gum that focus on passing the gum, maneuvering without dropping the gum, etc.

7. Re-run the obstacle course and time it.

8. Compare your results with the first run and process the differences between timed runs #1 and #2.

9. Emphasize that making mistakes gives us a chance to grow and practicing an unfamiliar skill can lead to improvement.

### MATERIALS NEEDED

- Wrapped pieces of bubble gum or small bubble gum balls
- Plastic spoons (one per student)
- Markers
- Score Sheet
- Stop watch or clock with second hand

# My Famous Flop!

## OBJECTIVE

Students will identify a time when they experienced a flop or failure and discuss what they did about it.

## DIRECTIONS

Share a story with the students about a time you flopped (did not experience success at something). It could be anything from making a cake that turned out poorly to trying a new skill out for the first time (if you have pictures, like a "Pinterest Fail," share with the students).

FOR EXAMPLE: When I was in 7th grade cooking class, we were making blueberry muffins. The recipe called for one teaspoon of salt and I put in one tablespoon. The muffins tasted terrible, but I have never confused teaspoon with tablespoon since!

**MATERIALS NEEDED**
- One paper plate per student folded in half
- Markers/crayons
- Video camera or phone (optional)
- Writing paper

1. Allow students to ask questions about your experience.

2. Have students brainstorm in small groups and identify an experience when they did not have first-time success at something, and flopped.

3. Have students draw a picture of the flop on the top half of the paper plate and write about what they learned from flopping on the bottom half of the paper plate. Encourage kids to use photos (i.e., arm in cast) or even recreate the flop through video.

4. Encourage students to share their flops with the class. Include time for students to ask questions:
   - When you flopped, did you give up?
   - What did you do so that you wouldn't flop again?
   - What did you learn from flopping?
   - Did you have to get help from someone else?

**Display paper plates around classroom for all to see and celebrate FLOPPING!!!!**

# Thomas "Bubble Gum Brain" Edison!

## INTRODUCTION

Thomas Edison was the inventor of many things and was extremely accomplished. He had a strong work ethic, and was determined not to give up. His perseverance and positive attitude helped him overcome great obstacles and challenges. While working to perfect the light bulb, Edison was unstoppable in his experimentation, which led to thousands of unsuccessful trials. But he took this learning in stride and is quoted as saying "I have not failed. I've just found 10,000 ways that won't work." Thomas Edison had a bubble gum brain!

## OBJECTIVE

Students will study and evaluate growth mindset quotes by Thomas Edison and find ways to apply them to their own thinking process.

## MATERIALS NEEDED

- Thomas Edison quotes sheet
- Blank letter sized paper (one per student)
- Markers, colored pencils, crayons

## DIRECTIONS

1. Pass out the Thomas Edison quote sheet (next page) and have kids discuss the meaning and interpretation of each quote in small groups of three or four.

2. Have each student choose one quote that fits him/her best and design a poster promoting that quote.

3. Have each student share their posters with the class.

4. Display the posters on a Thomas "Bubble Gum Brain" Edison bulletin board for all to enjoy, apply, and learn from.

5. OPTIONAL: can award prizes for the most creative, most fun, and most fitting quotes.

# Thomas Edison Quotes

*I never did anything by accident, nor did any of my inventions come by accident, they came by work.*

*Many of life's failures are people who did not realize how close they were to success when they gave up.*

*I am not discouraged because every wrong attempt discarded is another step forward.*

*To invent you need a good imagination and pile of junk.*

*Discontent is the first necessity of progress.*

*Our greatest weakness lies in giving up. The most certain way to succeed is always to try just one more time.*

*The first requisite for success is the ability to apply your physical and mental energies to one problem incessantly without growing weary.*

*The three great essentials to achieve anything worthwhile are first, hard work; second, stick-to-it-ness; and third; common sense.*

*Genius is 1% inspiration and 99% perspiration.*

*We shall have no better conditions in the future if we are satisfied with all those which we have at present.*

# Mindset Journals

## OBJECTIVE

Students will journal about goals, struggles and successes they have had along the way.

## DIRECTIONS

1. Pass out a notebook to each student and allow them to decorate the cover in a way that uniquely represents their growth mindset (i.e., a bubble gum brain, rubber bands, words like "Anything is Possible,"etc.).

2. Read a few entries from your personal journal that emulate the value of having a growth mindset. Explain that an journal entry can vary in length, look (could be a picture), and content.

3. Designate a "Growth Mindset Journal Time" for students each day (around 15 minutes). Let students know that these are their personal journals and they DO NOT need to share what they write with others unless they choose to do so.

4. Each week, allow students who want to share the opportunity to read one entry from their journal. Leave time at the end for group comments and questions.

5. Explain to students how going back over previous journal entries can help them track the progress they are making in growing their mindset.

NOTE: You may want to use a daily growth mindset prompt to inspire your students to think out loud on paper.

## MATERIALS NEEDED

- A notebook for each student
- Markers, colored pencils, or crayons
- Teacher's Journal
  NOTE: Teacher should start a journal ahead of time showing how some entries can benefit the development of a growth mindset.

# Design Your Own "Bubble Gum Brain" T-Shirt!

## OBJECTIVE

Students will use their creativity to design a t-shirt that visualizes a bubble gum brain mentality.

## DIRECTIONS

1. Pre-dye all t-shirts so they are pink (optional)

2. Give each student a template.

3. Have students first practice designing their t-shirt on the paper template using markers, colored pencils, crayons, etc.

4. Using the fabric markers or paints, have students draw and color their designs on the actual t-shirt. Set aside for at least 24 hours to dry completely.

5. Allow time for students to explain the significance of their design to the rest of the class.

6. Designate periodic BGB T-shirt days!

## MATERIALS NEEDED

- T-shirt (kids can bring an old one from home)
- T-shirt paper template
- Markers (permanent or fabric), colored pencils, waterproof fabric paint
- Pink dye (optional)

# Famous Bubble Gum Brains

## MATERIALS NEEDED

- Biographies, books, and articles about famous people
- Computer time to conduct supervised internet searches
- One information sheet per student

## OBJECTIVE

Students will research famous people who have shown a growth mindset in becoming successful.

## DIRECTIONS

1. Have students choose a celebrity, athlete, political figure, or role model they admire (can have students work solo, in pairs, or groups).

2. Research the life of that person and look for times when he/she used a growth mindset to accomplish success or personal goals.

3. Have each student or team complete the information sheet (below) on their person.

4. Using the completed information sheet, have each student or team write a paper explaining what their chosen person did to achieve success, how they learned from their mistakes, and how having a bubble gum brain helped them along the way.

5. Share stories with the rest of the class and display along with a picture of their chosen person.

- - - - - - - - - - - - - - - - - - - - - - - - - - - - - - - - - - - - - - - - - - - - - - - - - - - - - - - - - - -

Name(s):_____

My Chosen Person is: _____

He/she is famous because:_____

_____

### BACKGROUND INFORMATION

Where did he/she grow up? What was their family like?_____

_____

What jobs has this person had throughout his/her life? _____

_____

Times he/she has struggled and why? _____

_____

People who encouraged my famous person: _____

_____

Examples of how he/she has used a growth mindset (or bubble gum brain) to accomplish their goals: _____

_____

What has this person taught me about having a growth mindset?_____

# Bubble Gum Blowing Contest

## OBJECTIVE

Students will apply growth mindset skills while trying to blow the biggest bubble.

**MATERIALS NEEDED**

- Sugar-free bubble gum
- Phone or video camera
- Packs of gum for the winning team
- Marker board or chalkboard
- Comments Sheet (next page)

## DIRECTIONS

1. Explain to the class that they will be having a bubble gum blowing contest to see who can blow the largest bubble.

2. Put kids into groups of three to four.

3. Give each student 1or 2 pieces of sugar-free bubble gum.

4. Allow students time to prepare their gum and practice blowing.

5. Listen for and write down all comments/statements you hear from the kids throughout this activity. (Note: you may want another adult in the room to do this while the activity is taking place).

6. Evaluate one group at a time and choose the biggest bubble blower, while the other groups chew their gum quietly.

7. Group finalists together and have them compete while one student video tapes and/or takes pictures of the event.

8. Encourage each group of four to cheer on their finalist.

9. Declare your class winner!

10. Read and review the comments that were made by students throughout the activity and categorize them appropriately on the board for all to see.

11. Discuss comments as a class and see if Fixed Mindset comments could have been stated in more positive ways and made into Growth Mindset comments. Reiterate the importance of having a growth mindset.

12. Give a pack of gum to the following winners:
    - The "Stickiest Mess" Award
    - The "Stick With It" Award
    - The "Stretch Your Mind" Award
    - The "Good Sport" Award
    - The "Great Encourager" Award

NOTE: The result (blowing the biggest bubble) is not rewarded…it's the process that really matters.

## GROWTH Mindset Comments

_____

_____

_____

_____

_____

_____

_____

_____

_____

_____

_____

_____

_____

_____

_____

_____

_____

## FIXED Mindset Comments

_____

_____

_____

_____

_____

_____

_____

_____

_____

_____

_____

_____

_____

_____

_____

_____

_____

# Magic Mindset Milk!

## OBJECTIVE

Students will see in a concrete way how the factors contributing to a growth mindset can blend together magically inside their head.

NOTE: You can search "milk, food coloring, and dish soap" on YouTube to see how people have done this experiment.

**MATERIALS NEEDED**

- Clear baking dish or pie plate
- One gallon of milk
- 4-5 drops of dishwashing liquid
- Q-Tips
- Food coloring (green, blue, red, and yellow)

## DIRECTIONS

1. Assign each color to represent the following:

   - Expecting the best of myself – Green
   - Working hard – Red
   - Becoming more resilient – Blue
   - Being open-minded – Yellow
   - Being GRITTY and never, EVER giving up! – Orange
   - Label the soap "Growth Mindset Enhancer"

2. Pour enough milk in the pan so that the pan is about ½ full.

3. Carefully place several drops of food coloring onto the surface of the milk.

4. Explain that each color is vital to developing a growth mindset.

5. Dip a Q-Tip into the dish soap and stick it straight down into the colors. As the colors begin to explode, explain that, just like the colors, when we use our brain to think big, anything is possible!

# You Can Learn A Lot From A Baby!

## OBJECTIVE

Students will see that we are all born with a growth mindset and a baby learning to walk for the first time is a great example of that.

## DIRECTIONS

1. Have students watch videos of babies who are learning to walk for the first time and take notes about what they see.

2. Discuss the following questions with students:

   • What do you think goes through a baby's head when it falls down?
   • Do you think babies have a growth mindset or a fixed mindset? Why?
   • What did you learn about your own mindset by watching this?

   • How old were you when you started to have a fixed mindset in a certain area? What is it (i.e. school, going to college, playing an instrument, etc.)?
   • Why do you think it happened?
   • What can you do to change it?

# You Can GROW Your Intelligence!

## OBJECTIVE

Students will understand that the brain is like a muscle…the more exercise it gets, the stronger, and more effective it becomes.

**MATERIALS NEEDED**

• Copies of the article "You Can Grow Your Intelligence" (link: http://bit.ly/2vw98oI)
• YouTube videos – search "You Can Grow Your Intelligence" (link: http://bit.ly/2vvRpxR)
• "Brain Teaser" activities and games, Mensa workbooks
• Crayons, colored pencils, or markers

## DIRECTIONS

1. Make a copy of the article for each student and read it aloud together, then discuss.

2. Show a few of the videos and reiterate what was shared in the article via a classroom discussion.

3. Give students time to challenge themselves and each other with puzzles and worksheets. Who surprised themselves by accomplishing something they didn't think they could?

# Bubble Gum Brain Phrase Find

## MATERIALS NEEDED
- Phrase sheet
- Pencil or pen

## OBJECTIVE

Students will recognize the difference between growth mindset phrases and fixed mindset phrases.

## DIRECTIONS

1. Pass a phrase sheet out to each student.
2. Explain that growth mindset phrases focus on praising the effort or the process…not the results or ability.
3. Have students circle all of the growth mindset phrases.
4. Correct/dispute/process answers as a class.

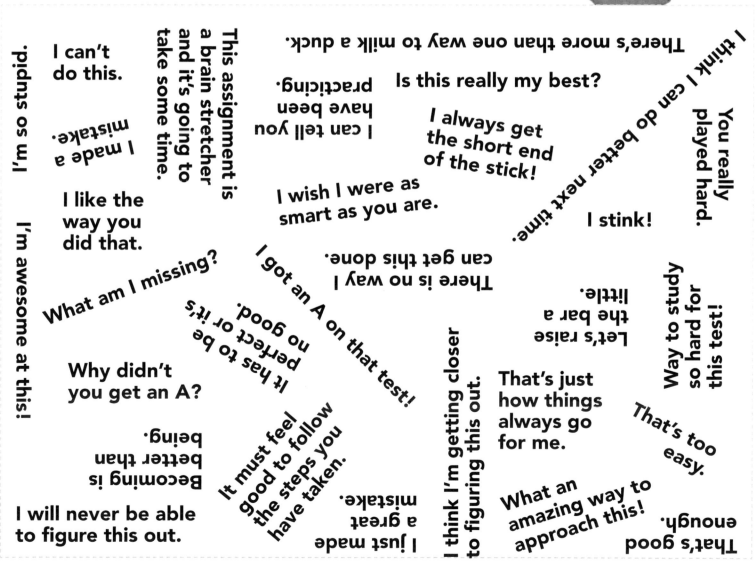

I can't do this.

I'm so stupid.

I made a mistake.

This assignment is a brain stretcher and it's going to take some time.

There's more than one way to milk a duck.

I can tell you have been practicing.

Is this really my best?

I think I can do better next time.

You really played hard.

I always get the short end of the stick!

I like the way you did that.

I wish I were as smart as you are.

I stink!

I'm awesome at this!

What am I missing?

There is no way I can get this done.

I got an A on that test!

It has to be perfect or it's no good.

Way to study so hard for this test!

Let's raise the bar a little.

Why didn't you get an A?

That's just how things always go for me.

That's too easy.

Becoming is better than being.

It must feel good to follow the steps you have taken.

I just made a great mistake.

I think I'm getting closer to figuring this out.

What an amazing way to approach this!

I will never be able to figure this out.

That's good enough.

# Water Bottle, Water Bottle, What Will You Be?

## OBJECTIVE

Students will use growth mindset strategies to think of and create another use for a disposable plastic water bottle.

## DIRECTIONS

1. Have each student bring an empty disposable water bottle from home. Explain that students need to use their bubble gum brains and the provided materials to create another use for their water bottles.

2. Allow students to work in pairs or groups and brainstorm ideas, then work solo in designing the new use for their water bottles.

3. Upon completion, have each student share their creation with the rest of the class. Celebrate the resourcefulness and creativity used in stretching their minds.

## MATERIALS NEEDED

- Empty plastic water bottle with lid
- Hot glue gun
- Scissors
- Misc. craft supplies (construction paper, stickers, pipe cleaners, craft sticks, etc.)

# Tease Your Brain

## OBJECTIVE

Students will have the opportunity to work together in small groups and develop their growth mindset by thinking through brain teaser problems.

## MATERIALS NEEDED

- Several brain teaser problems written out on individual cards (search the internet for appropriate mindbender problems found on sites such as Cool Math 4 Kids, Fun Brain Teasers, and Mind Bending Logic).
- Hat or basket to put cards in
- Paper and pencils
- Manipulatives

## DIRECTIONS

1. Search for appropriate mindbender problems online and copy them onto individual cards. Fold all cards and place in a hat or basket.

2. Put students into groups of three or four.

3. Have one member of each group draw a mindbender problem out of the hat.

4. Encourage each group to use growth mindset strategies and their bubble gum brains to solve the mindbender problems.

5. Remind students of the Bubble Gum Brain oath as they are working on the problems:

   - I will **Expect the best from myself.**
   - I will **Work hard and try new things.**
   - I will **Become more resilient.**
   - I will **Be open-minded.**
   - I will **Be GRITTY and never, EVER give up!!!**

6. Allow students to present their problem and solution to the class. Celebrate teamwork and resilience.

NOTE: If a group cannot solve their mindbender problem, try to work together as a class to solve it.

# Bubble Gum Brain Rap

## OBJECTIVE

Students will use phrases from the book *Bubble Gum Brain* to create and perform raps that encourage others to develop a growth mindset.

### MATERIALS NEEDED

- *Bubble Gum Brain* storybook by Julia Cook (NCYI  2017)
- Rhyming and/or meaningful sections of the book (phrase sheet see below)
- Pencil/pen and paper

## DIRECTIONS

1. Put students into groups of three or four.
2. Read the book *Bubble Gum Brain* aloud to the students and discuss what it means to have a growth mindset.
3. Pass out phrase sheets (below).
4. Have kids write and perform *Bubble Gum Brain* raps that include phrases from the book.

---

**I just can't figure this out Yet.**

**"I realize now that my mindset's been stuck.
I was caught up in what I was "seeing."
Now I know I must look outside the box,
because becoming is better than being."**

**I need
to make
some great
mistakes.**

**Grow and hope and stretch and bend.**

**"It's not about how much talent you have or how much stuff you can do.**

**Here I go again.**

**What matters most is how hard you work at becoming a better you!"**

**Just try.**

**Add a YET to every "I can't" that you have.**

---

# Tease Your Brain

## OBJECTIVES

Students will experience and discuss the process of trial and error and learn the meaning of The Power of YET!

## DIRECTIONS

1. Give each student 15 playing cards.

2. Show them a picture of what a house of cards looks like. Give them a good look, and then put the picture away.

3. Set a timer for five minutes.

4. Have students attempt to build a self-standing house of cards using all 15 cards.

5. While attempts are being made, record some of the words that are being said, i.e.:

    a. This is impossible!

    b. This stinks!

    c. I can't do this!

    d. There is no way!

    After the five minutes are over, discuss how it felt to try, and what you heard and observed. Did some give up right away? Were there a few who kept trying the entire time?

6. Introduce the Power of YET!

    "I can't build a house of cards! " vs. "I can't build a house of cards YET!"

7. Show video (on YouTube) – How to Build an Awesome and Easy House of Cards (link: http://bit.ly/2lTU0sp).

8. Allow kids another five minutes to try again.

9. As a class, start and stop the video a third time and have students attempt to build their house of cards as they watch short sections of the video.

10. Discuss how important trial and error become when solving a problem.

## MATERIALS NEEDED

- Picture of a simple house made out of cards (find on Google Images)
- Several decks of cards (you will need 15 playing cards for each student)
- YouTube video: How To Build an Awesome and Easy House of Cards

# Becoming is BETTER than Being!

## OBJECTIVE

Students will experience how becoming is better than being.

## DIRECTIONS

1. Have students unwrap one piece of gum and start chewing it.

2. Discuss how chewing the gum activates their brain (taste, smell, movement, coordination, not biting their tongue, etc.)

3. Have each student use pipe cleaners to build two stick figure bodies (see YouTube video "How to Make a Stick Figure Out of a Pipe Cleaner").

4. Using the glue stick, glue each pipe cleaner body onto a 3 X 5 card.

5. Using the glue gun, attach a wrapped piece of gum to the top of one of the bodies to form a brick brain head.

6. Glue googly eyes on the brick brain.

7. Spit out your wad of gum and wash it off in cold water and then hot glue it to the top of the other pipe cleaner body to form a bubble gum brain head.

8. Glue googly eyes onto the gum and let dry overnight.

9. Spray bubble gum brain with clear coat and dry thoroughly.

10. Staple all brick brains onto one bulletin board and all bubble gum brains on another bulletin board, leaving room in the center of each bulletin board.

11. Research online both growth mindset and fixed mindset sayings and write them on the bulletin boards in the center of each group of stick people.

12. Discuss with students how creating a bubble gum brain stick figure is much more fun than creating a brick brain stick figure.

### MATERIALS NEEDED

- Pipe Cleaners
- 3 X 5 Blank Index Cards – two per student
- Googly eyes (four per student)
- Glue gun
- Glue stick
- Clear coat spray paint or shellac
- Bubble Gum (wrapped and shaped in a cube) – 2 pieces per student
- Miscellaneous growth mindset and fixed mindset statements (see examples below)